Clovis Keeps His Cool

*In loving memory of Gramma Dee
and with gratitude to Jen B.*
— K. A.

Thanks to my friend Artyom for the inspiration.
— E. F.

Text copyright © 2021 Katelyn Aronson. Illustrations copyright © 2021 Eve Farb. First published in 2021 by Page Street Kids, an imprint of Page Street Publishing Co., 27 Congress Street, Suite 105, Salem, MA 01970, www.pagestreetpublishing.com. All rights reserved. No part of this book may be reproduced or used, in any form or by any means, electronic or mechanical, without prior permission in writing from the publisher. Distributed by Macmillan, sales in Canada by The Canadian Manda Group. ISBN-13: 978-1-64567-213-5. ISBN-10: 1-64567-213-1. CIP data for this book is available from the Library of Congress. This book was typeset in Amasis Std. The illustrations were done digitally. Cover and book design by Julia Tyler for Page Street Kids. Printed and bound in Shenzhen, Guangdong, China
21 22 23 24 25 CCO 5 4 3 2 1

Page Street Publishing uses only materials from suppliers who are committed to responsible and sustainable forest management. Page Street Publishing protects our planet by donating to nonprofits like The Trustees, which focuses on local land conservation.

Clovis Keeps His Cool

Katelyn Aronson   illustrated by Eve Farb

PAGE
STREET
KiDS

Clovis ran his granny's old china shop in the town square.

On inventory day, he unpacked
and stacked porcelain so fine,
you could almost see through it.

Never did he drop one dish.

"'Grace, grace. Nothing broken to replace,'" he whispered,
"as Granny used to say."

There was just one problem.
Clovis had a temper as big as he was.

As a linebacker for the Cloverdale Chargers,
he'd lost his temper on

and off the field.

But since taking over Granny's shop, he felt calmer.
Until the day a few old rival players dropped by . . .

Not them, Clovis thought. He clenched his teeth.

"Well looky here!" said one. "The bull in the china shop!"
"Is THAT 'Colossal' Clovis?" said another. "I hardly recognized him in the apron!"

"Yeah, he quit football to play 'tea party,'"
said the third. "What a **WIMP!**"

Clovis clenched his teeth.
The anger rose—that old urge to charge.
But he resisted.

He breathed in on a count of ten.

1-2-3-4-5-6-7-8-9-10

He breathed out.

"I will not lose my cool," Clovis said.

Tired of waiting for a response,
the hecklers moved on.

On dusting day, Clovis put on soothing music.
He spent a while in lotus position, then set to work.

"GRAAAAACE, GRAAAACE.

Nothing broken to replaaaaace," he sang,
and soon the glassware gleamed.

Until voices rose over the violins . . .

Not again, Clovis thought.

"You missed a spot!" said one.
"Better watch that big behind!"
said another.

"HAHA!"

"Yeah. One false move and . . .

CRASH!"

said the third.

Clovis clenched his teeth.
There it was again—
that urge to charge.

But he resisted.

Quickly, he grabbed a fluffy cushion
to squeeze. (Oops! That was the cat.
He stroked her instead.)

"I will not lose my cool," Clovis said.

Bored, the hecklers finally gave up
and headed home.

On display day, Clovis lit a lavender-scented candle.
He sipped some chamomile tea, then set to work.

"Grace.

Grace.

Nothing. Broken.

To replace," he chanted,
installing the window decor.

Until noses nuzzled the glass . . .

This time, they barged into his shop.
"Fancy a spot of tea, fellas?" said one.
"Oh, isn't that *pwecious!* A portrait of his granny?" said another.
"Wow," said the third. "I didn't know she had a beard!"

Clovis was a kettle, about to boil over. How dare they insult Granny?

They picked up Granny's once-favorite teacup and taunted him.
"Hey, Clovis, can you still catch a pass?"

"No!" cried Clovis. "Don't!"
He turned too late.

SMASH!

Granny's cup lay in bits at his hooves.

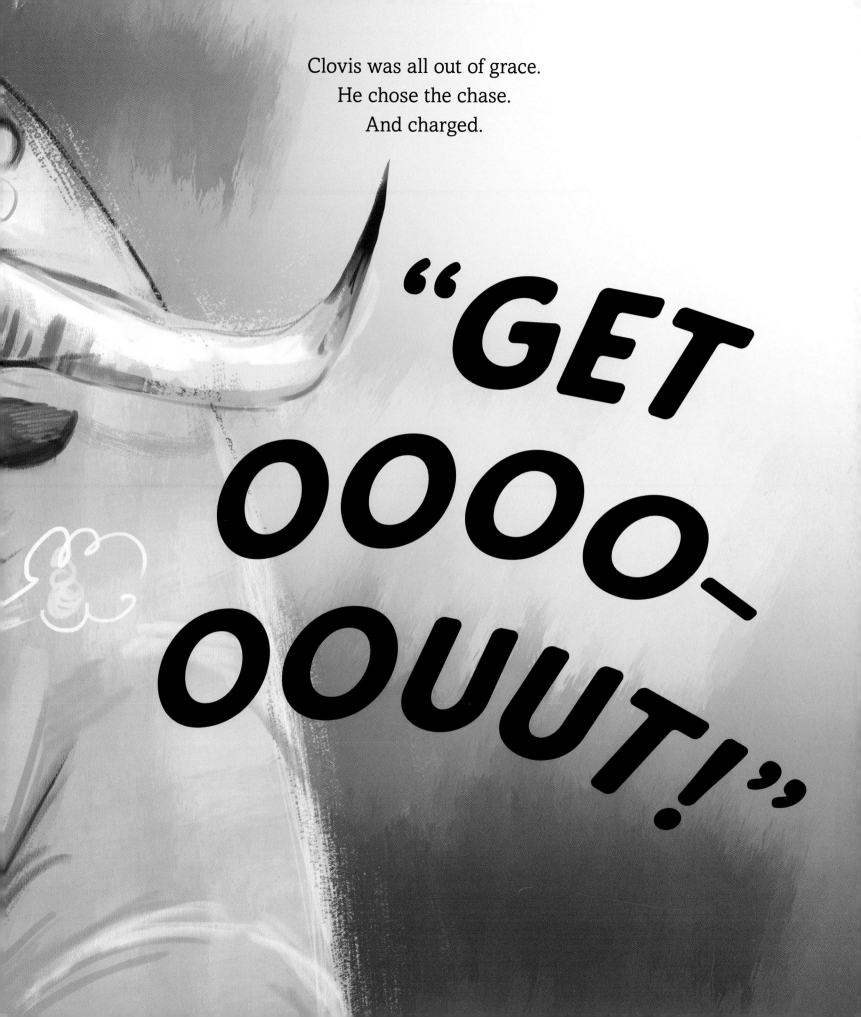

Clovis was all out of grace.
He chose the chase.
And charged.

"GET
OOOO-
OOUUT!"

Clovis tore through town, hot on the hecklers' hooves. The stampede didn't stop until he'd chased them to the end of a dark alley. The hecklers huddled together, trembling. This was the Clovis they remembered. The one capable of crushing anything. Anyone.

Clovis snorted and pawed the ground.
He lowered his horns to strike . . .

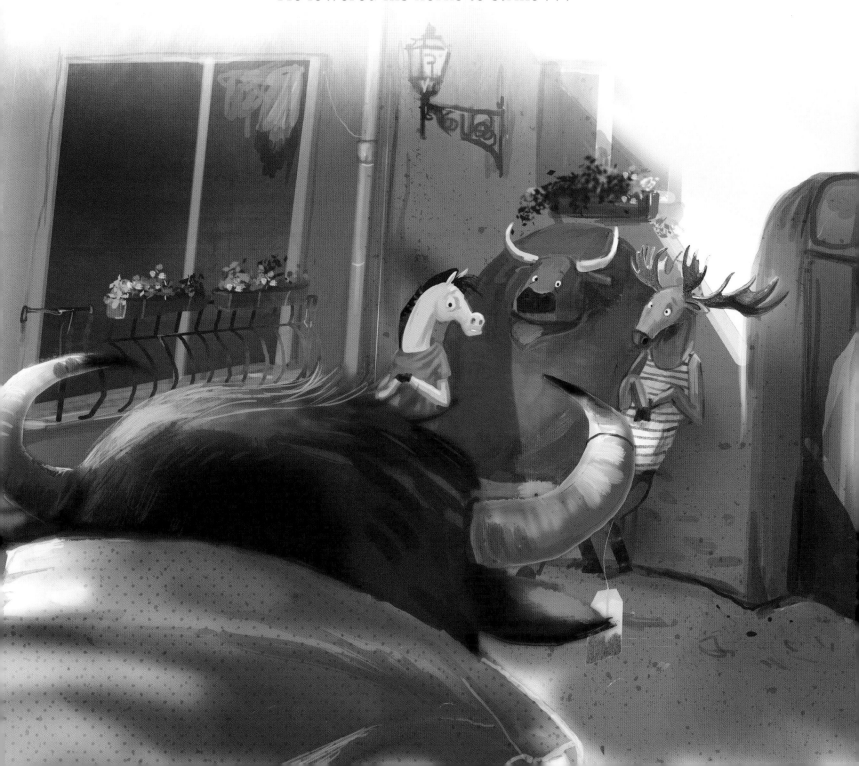

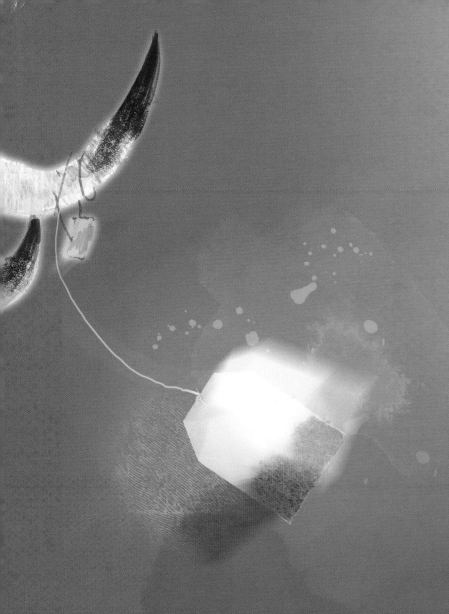

. . . and one tiny tea bag dropped into view. Clovis stopped.

Granny! he thought. *Oh, Granny Grace! Everything's broken.*
Your teacup. Your shop.

From somewhere deep in Clovis's memory, Granny's voice answered:
My dear . . . Grace. Grace. What is broken can be replaced.

Clovis let her gentle words wash over him.

He looked straight at his enemies and sighed.
"Look, I may be a bull. But I'm no *bully*.
Could I interest you guys in . . . a cup of tea?"

The hecklers looked at each other in disbelief.
But Clovis seemed serious. So serious,
that when he turned to lead the way, they followed.

Back at the shop, the window and its wares lay
smashed to smithereens. Clovis set a table anyways.
Carefully, he poured four cups of tea.
And together, they sat in silence, sipping.

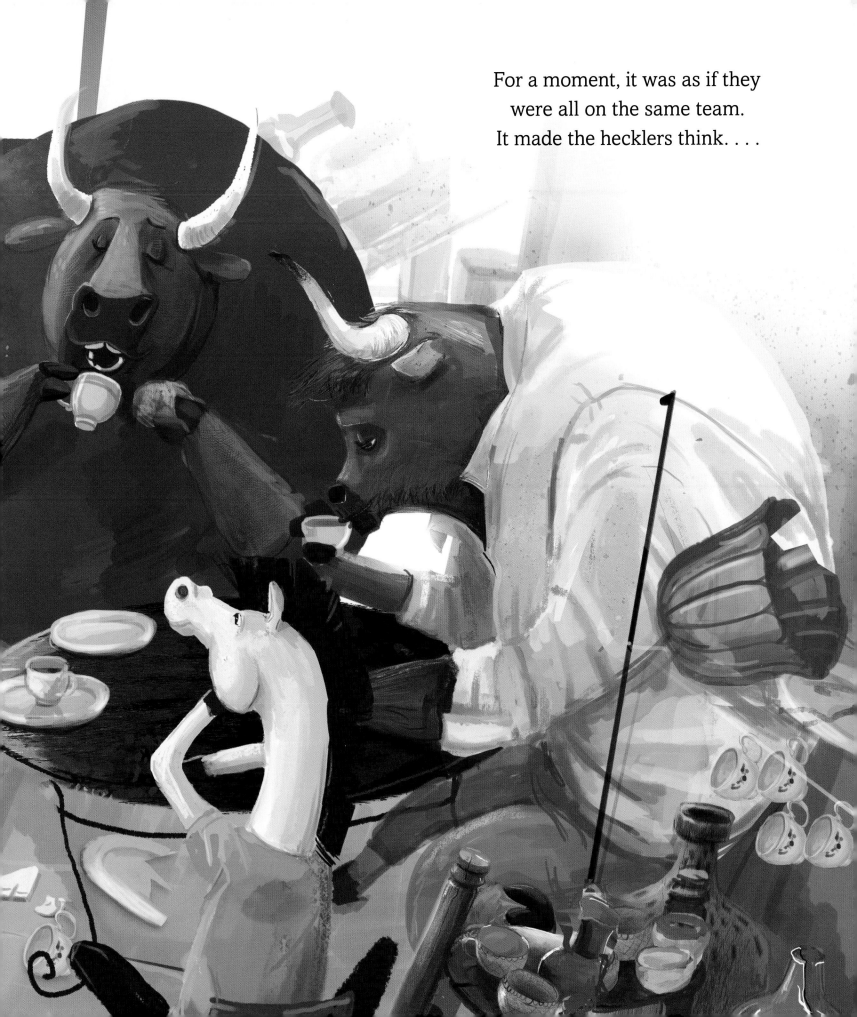

For a moment, it was as if they
were all on the same team.
It made the hecklers think. . . .

The next day, they came back. *Oh no,* Clovis thought.

But this time was different.

They came back the next day,
and the next.

Little by little, they helped Clovis
pick up the pieces, putting right
what had gone wrong. And always,
Clovis served tea.

By the time his shop reopened, a few things had changed.
Clovis had old hobbies,

new friends,

and plenty of grace to go around.